S0-AFJ-529

Wouldn't You Like to Know

ALSO BY PAMELA PAINTER

Getting to Know the Weather
The Long and Short of It
What If? Writing Exercises for Fiction Writers
    (co-authored with Anne Bernays)

Pamela Painter

Wouldn't You Like to Know

very short stories

For Alexandria —
One of my very favorite
former students — well on
your way to wonderful
success. Do keep in touch
Warmly,
Pam Painter
2010

Carnegie Mellon University Press
Pittsburgh 2010

Acknowledgments

Stories have been published and reprinted as follows: "Your Letter in an Envelope in the Mail" in *Quick Fiction*; "Addictions and/or Appetites" in *Night Train*; "A View: 'Office at Night'" in *Smoke Long Quarterly*; "The New Year" in *Sundog*; *Southeast Review*, *Micro Fiction*, *Sudden Stories* and recorded on NPR *"Morning Stories"*; "Toasters" in *Mid-American Review* and *Flash Fiction Forward*; "Sick of Her Life" in *Quick Fiction*; "Dreamwork" in *Special Report*; "Snap Judgment" in *Quick Fiction*; "Twins" in *Sundog*, *Southeast Review*.

"Wouldn't You Like to Know" printed as "Family Therapy" in *Vestal Review*, *You Have Time For This*, and *Best American Flash Fiction of the 21st Century*; "Numb Enough" in *Iron Horse Literary Review*; "God" in *StoryQuarterly* and *Sudden Stories*; "Wyeth Drama: The Missing Scenes" in *The Short Story*; "Nose Interview" in *Iron Horse Literary Review*; "Ice" in *Mid-American Review*; "Air Show" in *Del Sol Review*; "Inside Job" in *Field Guide to Writing Flash Fiction*; "Clean" in *Iron Horse Literary Review*.

"Dud" in *Harvard Review*; "Not a Ghost Story" in *Vestal Review*; "First Night of Married Life" in *Quick Fiction*; "Driver's Test" published as "Skid Marks" in *Quarterly West*; "Put to Sleep" in *Narrative*; "Never Before" in *Quick Fiction*; "My Honey" in *The LA Review*; "Touchdown" in *Cape Cod Voice*; "Chance Encounter at LAX" in *Iron Horse Literary Review*.

Library of Congress Control Number 2009941179
ISBN 978-0-88748-527-5
Copyright © 2010 by Pamela Painter
All Rights Reserved
Printed and bound in the United States of America

10 9 8 7 6 5 4 3 2 1

CONTENTS

PART ONE

PART TWO

PART THREE

Part One

Your Letter in an Envelope
in the Mail

I never expected to see your handwriting again, but I'd recognize it anywhere even after all these years. A short letter, but it is oddly all still there. The frenetic, unpredictable hodgepodge of printing and script. The narcissism of the ornate capital letters—except for your lazy disinclination to flow with the capital F when a demonstrably intelligent right angle will do. The jovial belly of the lowercase f, the fat loops of the lowercase g, q, j, p, and y spreading exuberance, chatting up the line below. The ungenerous rendering of contained vowels. The dots of the i often off elsewhere. Your emphatic crossed t's—mirroring the dash of all those mad dashes. The parsimonious h—more like a t and needing a revised stroke to provide its rounded tummy. Oh you revised. And now? In spite of the way we parted years ago, tell me when and where—no, write me a note, another note with date and time and place. If I am still affected by your hand, I'll come.

Appetites and Addictions

I. Doing My Man

Her hands break my heart. I used to rent THE ROSE once a week and fast forward to the frames where the camera also loves her hands. Toward the end of the film, there she is at what should be her moment of triumph—she's come home to play the sold-out football stadium in her hometown, arrived with stage sets and lights, backup bands, roadies and groupies, the whole damn show. She can outdazzle the most popular girl, easily win away the handsome quarterback, oh she can sing.

But where is she—she is in a fluorescent-on-fire phone booth screwing the top off a bottle of bourbon, the bourbon a transluscent liquid like air and by now as necessary to her as breathing. Her slender fingers are so practiced in the hold, turn release of the bottle's top—hold, turn, release—that she can do it with trembling fingers, she can do it with her eyes closed, with her mouth touching, moaning into the phone.

Her mouth is wet, glistening, the liquor stings as her

tongue catches everything, and we follow her long swallows, but it is still her hands that the camera loves. Hold, turn, release. The pressure of her thumb and three fingers is so sure and graceful that not one revolution is ever lost. The pads of her fingers touch just above the top's rim, as if in boundaries the rim is everything. Oh Rose, you could have had it all.

You could have declined that needle, played to that rim for a while longer. Over and over, around and above that rim. You had a taste for love.

My fingers know all about it.

I hold him and turn and turn, back and forth, holding, turning, releasing. I am breathing him in, swallowing him. Closing him down. My fingers can break his heart.

II. Next Comes Soup

Not right after, no, but soon, I leave him where I did him and go to the kitchen to shift and clatter my pots and pans. Another satisfying sound that has to do with appetite. Sweet butter, a virgin oil and chopped onions are sizzling away in a heavy pot before I have to decide which soup? This might be about soup. This might be about me and my man.

I consider black bean, or roasted eggplant and garlic, or a warm Vichyssoise, or I could just as easily slide the pot off the burner, turn down the gas and have him do me again. I stop stirring for one long moment to think about this. I think about this scenario the way I sometimes think about falling asleep with his fingers inside me, my back curved into him, my bottom leg straight, my top leg bent at the knee and pulled in toward my damp breasts, pulled impossibly high.

The dense smell of onions softening in foaming butter keeps me with the soup.

Soup—what soup?

The butternut squash glows on the windowsill. I palm

the round base of the squash and peel its narrow throat. Then I hold the long moist throat and peel its hard curve. Chicken broth floats the onions for seconds before I bury them under a peeled tart apple, all that chopped squash. Not quite too late I add cumin, turmeric, cardamom, and thyme. This is going to take awhile, this soup. Later, I'll blend it smooth and serve it to my man with a cold dollop of sour cream and a baguette we'll acquire on a stroll to the corner bakery. For now he's not exactly waiting, but he's still in bed.

So. I'll adjust the heat, turn the flame low under the soup. Then I'll stand beside the bed. "I'm making soup," I'll say. And he'll say, "Hmmm, soup." I'll hold my fingers to his nose and he'll close his eyes and breathe in the onions. I'll tell him apples and cardamom and cumin and squash. "Maybe add a bit of ginger," he'll say, opening his eyes.

He'll pull me down, press my fingers to his mouth and his mouth will slowly open, opening me all over again. His wet sharp teeth and firm tongue will nibble the length of my fingers, swell the cup of my palm, ply the silent art of appetite. He'll teach me all of his. I'll teach him all of mine.

A View: *Office at Night*

They don't seem to be working, though up to a few minutes ago she was filing papers. A man (whom we assume is her boss) sits reading a page at his desk, holding it beneath a green banker's light. Her plump right arm bends to encompass a generous bosom and her right hand rests on the edge of the open file drawer. Perhaps seconds ago she turned toward the man at the desk. Her face is vulnerable, intent. She is waiting. A piece of paper, partly hidden by the desk, lies on the floor between her and the man. We are led to believe that Edward Hopper is in a train, passing by on the El.

A voluptuous curve—perhaps the most voluptuous curve in all of Hopper's paintings, almost to a surreal degree—belongs to this secretary in the night-blue dress in *Office at Night*, an oil on canvas, 1940. What word, in 1940, would have been used to describe those rounded globes beneath the stretch, from rounded hip to hip, of her blue dress.

If it weren't for that piece of paper on the floor, we might believe the museum's prim description of this painting. It says: "The secretary's exaggerated sexualized persona contrasts with the buttoned-up indifference of her boss; the frisson of their intimate overtime is undermined by a sense that the scene's erotic expectations are not likely to be met."

Indifference? Wrong. The man is far too intent on the paper he is reading—and he is not sitting head-on at his desk. He is somewhat tilted—toward the secretary. His mouth is slightly open as if to speak. His left ear is red. It is. It is red.

And what of their day. Her desk faces his in this small cramped office. He must have looked up from his papers to say to her, seated behind her black typewriter, that tonight they must stay late. Did she call her mother, or two roommates she met while attending Katherine Gibbs, to say her boss asked her to stay late. On other evenings, she would have finished dinner, perhaps been mending her stockings, or watching the newsreel at the cinema's double feature.

But here she is tonight, looking down at the paper on the floor. Was it she who dropped it? It is true that her dress has a chaste white collar, but the deep V of the neckline will surely fall open when she stoops over, perhaps bending at the knees over her spiffy black pumps, to retrieve the page. Another paper has been nudged toward the desk's edge and shows a refusal to lie flat in the slight breeze blowing the window shade into the office. Other papers are held in place by the 1940s black telephone, so heavy that in a forties noir film it might serve as the murder weapon.

Perhaps this story began at an earlier time. It might already be a situation, causing the young woman, just this morning, to choose to wear this particular blue dress. We are all in the middle of their drama. She will bend before him. Someone will turn off the lights. They will leave before midnight. Perhaps it won't turn out well. But for now the blue dress cannot be ignored.

PAMELA PAINTER

The New Year

It's late Christmas Eve at Spinelli's when Dominic presents us, the waitstaff, with his dumb idea of a bonus—Italian hams in casings so tight they shimmer like Gilda's gold lamé stockings.

At home, Gilda's waiting up for me with a surprise of her own: my stuff from the last three months is sitting on the stoop. Arms crossed, scarlet nails tapping the white satin sleeves of her robe, she says she's heard about Fiona. I balance the ham on my hip and pack my things—CDs, weights, a vintage Polaroid—into garbage bags she's provided free of charge. Then I let it all drop and offer up the ham in both hands, cradling it as if it might have been our child. She doesn't want any explanations—or the ham.

Fiona belongs to Dominic, and we are a short sad story of one night's restaurant despair. But the story's out and for sure I don't want Dominic coming after my ham.

Under Gilda's unforgiving eye, I sling my garbage bags into the trunk of the car and all Christmas day I drive with the radio off except when I call Gilda from a phone booth by the side of the road. Bing Crosby and me singing "White

Christmas" means nothing to her, so I head west, the ham glistening beside me in the passenger's seat. Somewhere in Indiana I strap it into a seat belt.

I stop to call again, but Gilda hangs up every time. After the next state, I send her pictures of my trip instead: The Ham under the silver arch of St. Louis; The Ham at the Grand Canyon; The Ham in Las Vegas. I'm taking a picture of The Ham in the Pacific when a big wave washes it out to sea. I send the picture anyway: The Ham in the Pacific Undertow. In this picture, you can't tell which of us is missing.

TOASTERS

The neighbors are at it again is what Joey says, just what his father would say if he were here. And just like his father, Joey shuts off all the lights, peels back the curtains over the sink, and settles in to watch the show.

The kitchen table is piled high with hot, dry laundry. I can fold it in the dark so I sit here listening to Joey describe what is flying out the Angelo's windows. So far it's plates, clothes, poker chips, and a fishing rod.

"Jesus, Mom, you're missing it. Mr. Angelo threw out the toaster. Wait'll Dad hears that." His excited sneakers thump the stove as he turns to ask if I remember when Mrs. Angelo flattened a whole row of my tomato plants with a bowling ball?

I tell him it's way past bedtime but he just gets his nose closer to the window to identify the next object and assess the damage. They keep lists—Joey and his father. Things thrown, sound effects made, and grievances screamed to the heavens as if to bring down a pre-apocalyptic condemnation.

Tonight it started with Mrs. Angelo's mother's weekend visits and moved on to Mr. Angelo's unfinished basement projects and early exits from his weekly poker game to parts and/or parties unknown. It is the same game my Harry has been losing too much money in for years and getting worse. The threadbare towels I'm folding are thin as silk and fold as flat.

"Wow," Joey says as Mrs. Angelo yowls one of her favorite four-letter words and the names of two forgiving saints. On purpose, I'm mismatching Harry's socks and thinking the exact same thing as Mrs. Angelo.

"Mom," Joey says, getting tired of the Angelo's show. "Where's Dad? Why isn't he home?"

Tonight I'll have to tell him. Because me and Harry. We're at it again too.

The streetlight from Joey's window glints on our toaster, plugged in and safe, and I think: me and Harry should take lessons from the Angelos. I admire the way they fight—everything flying out the windows and doors except the two of them.

Sick of Her Life

All summer, separated from her errant husband, the kids away at camp, all summer she brought men home from Mercer's Bar to her childhood summer cottage on the lake to avenge her husband's latest flings. One, two, nevermind—she'd finally settled on one man on the bar stool next to her, their final night of summer before she would return home to tell her husband what she thought. Labor Day weekend, the bar was slammed, the floor too sticky to dance, the sound racheted up ten notches. After four beers, she eyed the Gents' because some woman was locked in Ladies being sick of her life. She figured "Gents" would be a duplicate one-seater stall plus sink so she was shocked to see two men at urinals, three stalls without doors. Too late to exit. Jeans unzipped, panties down, she sat, helpless, disbelieving—as the housepainter, a Mercer's regular twice spurned, resentful, followed her in. The housepainter nodded to the two men gawking at it all, and reached behind him, his arm glistening with tiny dots of white paint, to hook the latch of the outside door. Then he moved across the cement floor to the front of her stall as if to say *you have what's coming*. Who would hear her cries for help above the jukebox's manic joy and sappy sorrow. Her last and final man was deep in talk about the Yankees' latest win. Who would wonder why the door to the Gents was latched? With dangerous desperation, she said, "OK. Let's have a peeing contest." She actually said "pee" not "piss," unable to stop her own hot stream. "Over there; line up. Now." In front of her, the housepainter hesitated, speckled menace shining on his arms, then he turned and joined the other men to pee his heart out. She finished, yanked up her jeans and hit the latch. There must be a better way to live her life.

DREAMWORK

Janek is lying on his back beside me. We are at the country home of Janek's friends who have gone to Prague for the summer. Nothing in this pale, spare room belongs to us except our clothes, my drawing board, and Janek's books. Every morning, the dull gleam of the brass bed startles me. The painted, stenciled floors are slick and cool. Outside the window, wisteria filters the morning light. Janek just told me his dream, an unlit cigarette held between two taut fingers. I heard his voice—curious, surprised. I heard my name, but I didn't listen. I was thinking of how I want to wake alone when we return to the city. But I don't know how to tell him. A dream is not the way.

"It's your turn," Janek says. He is smoking now. He exhales in that Eastern European way, allowing the smoke to drift from his parted lips. Only when he's angry does he purse his lips to blow a thin, ghostly stream toward the ceiling. He turns his head to me on the pillow. "What did you dream?"

"My turn." I adjust the sheets across my breasts and raise a knee. Eyes closed, I sift through what I dreamed for things to tell him, things to change.

I mention water because there was water. "It was hot, humid. I remember the heat." Janek's leg is pressing against me; our bodies are still damp from making love. "My arms were bare, and you weren't wearing a shirt. Or a belt, just rolled-up khakis. You were tanned like last summer, after Tenerife." I loved Janek last summer, but I love someone else now. Janek's suspicions are my fault. He deserves to know. Then, hurt, he will leave me in a polite, orderly fashion. He will smoke more for a while. But I'm a coward and now seems not the time for leaving someone you have loved.

"Where were we? Were we in Tenerife?" He lifts and smooths my long hair over his pillow.

"We were taking a trip in a rowboat."

"Rowboat?" He dislikes boats, water, national borders that drop rather than rise. I should have changed the rowboat.

"It was silver. Aluminum?" I look at him for confirmation of what a sleek, silver rowboat would be made of. He shrugs. Smoke settles onto his shoulders, my hair. I wash my hair every day now. Sometimes twice after I have been with Cal.

"And." His shoulder dips. He nudges me to continue.

I close my eyes again. You do not look at lovers when you are telling dreams. Dreams are for when you are side by side, perhaps driving, sometimes out walking, but mostly lying together in a rumpled bed. Janek spoke his dream to the low-beamed ceiling. I continue. "The water was a deep green because of all the reeds. The river was narrow, and we could see the reeds leaning toward us." I swish my hands on the sheets. "You were paddling, paddling hard against the current."

"Do you 'paddle' a boat," he asks?

"Well, maybe you were rowing. I remember the muscles of your arms, the way you leaned hard into the stroke." I am actually seeing him above me from moments ago.

"And?"

"We were going upriver for a picnic. I had packed a lunch of avocado sandwiches and Monchego cheese. When

PAMELA PAINTER

we pulled up to the bank, we were going to chill the wine in the river—wedge the bottle in with rocks. I had my sketch pad; you were working on a review."

"But where were we going?"

"Up the river."

"Is that it? That's all?"

"Let me think." Our hands stop swishing and rowing. He is in danger of drowning in my dream. I know he is listening for signs of Cal. We met Cal by accident last night at the opera where he sat several rows in front of us. He is my lover—rather he is the one I love. He is a man with the deliberate movements of a bird watcher, and from him I have learned to take slow, alert walks. Last night, even then, his opera glasses seemed poised as if for open air. "It was so hot that the birds on the shore were silent. I was watching for birds, for a quick flash of color, but they stayed hidden."

"Birds?" Janek moves his head on the pillow to look at me, but I don't open my eyes.

"We were identifying birds and flowers."

"Ah, flowers." He brings the cigarette to his lips and breathes deeply. It is this gesture—bringing his fingers slowly flat against his parted lips, his fingers touching his lips—that I have sketched over and over, a gesture I will miss and remember.

"Those reeds," I say. "Once, you stopped the boat and pulled great handfuls of reeds out of the water."

"Pulled . . . reeds." He snorts smoke, then stubs out his cigarette.

"You know. As if you were doing an arrangement." He often brings home one or two extravagant, exotic blooms. He has taught me about strange flowers that don't look like flowers, but rather like some ceramicist's art. Flowers one doesn't see on a walk. "Then we began to drift downstream, and you went back to paddling. Or rowing." My knee sways, making waves on the blue cotton sheet.

"Rowing," he says.

"I wasn't doing anything, just gliding along. I wasn't wearing sunglasses, but you were. I couldn't see your eyes. And you were sweating."

Janek has turned his back to me and is now propped on his elbow, rummaging for a match on the bedside table. The sheet has pulled away from my breasts. His back and buttocks are taut with reaching.

"You were dipping your hands into the water and pulling up reeds. You had to pull hard. They were slimy and tubular, like seaweed. Then you handed them to me as if they were a bouquet—or soup greens." I glance over at him and almost laugh.

He settles back against the pillow. "Just make them flowers," he suggests.

Abruptly I sit up and swing my legs over the side of the bed to the pale-green floor "I don't remember any more of the dream. I'm going to shower. You start the coffee for once."

But Janek turns and pulls me back down to the bed. We are both lying on my hair. Tears of surprise and pain fill my eyes. Our faces almost touch on his pillow. "You're lying about your dream," he says. "Why are you lying to me."

I touch his face, his lips. Then once again, I look away so that I can begin. "Let me tell you what I dreamed," I say. I will tell him about Cal, but first I will tell him my dream.

"I was alone in the rowboat," I say.

"Alone," says Janek. His voice hoarse from too many cigarettes.

"I was floating downriver, drifting toward an inlet where I was to meet someone, someone I have been seeing for the past month."

"Where was I?"

"I don't know. You weren't in the dream."

"Go on," Janek says, rising up on an elbow, catching my hair. "How does this dream end?" He inhales deeply and blows a tornado of smoke away from me.

"I pull the rowboat onto the bank. I spread a blanket and cool the wine."

"And?"

"But that's all," I say. I look at him, at his fingers flat against his mouth. "I was just waiting, waiting for someone to come."

"So, you know who you were waiting for," Janek says, watching me.

"Yes," I say, breathing in the wisteria and smoke.

"Oh, he'll be there," Janek says. "As soon as I am gone."

I turn to him, ready to tell him about Cal. But Janek gets out of bed now, out of our borrowed bed on borrowed time. As he dresses, gathers up his cigarettes and book, he tells me it was the reeds, the weeds, that told him just enough. There's nothing more to know.

Snap Judgment

"Two mice drowned in the toilet," he told her, then immediately he wondered what made him mention or even think of that? They were flat on their backs in his bed after making love. Languorously drying. It was the middle of the day. Ordinarily after sex he would be thinking of French toast, bacon, or smoked salmon and her soft-scrambled eggs with chives. The *Times*. "So I bought traps. Two traps. Three days later, I caught two more." The traps were those that snap. "Snap." He explained the virtue of snap versus poison or glue boards. Glue boards were cruel, poison also.

She pulled the covers up to her shoulders. "What do you have against mice?" she asked.

"Mouse turds in my skillets, and they gnaw the electric wiring and burn the house down. They carry disease. I'm up to number nine," he said.

"You?" she said, "you!" He felt her turn on her side to study him, the mouse murderer. "You know," she said. "There are statistics—ratios of mice caught to those still, so to speak, roaming free. In your house."

He knew almost everything but he didn't know this.

"For every mouse you kill—snap—you can be sure there are seven more flitting about your kitchen, nesting in the walls, doing what we're doing. Did." She lifted the covers to peek at their mutually satisfied selves. Then she continued, "A buck mouse can impregnate four doe mice in one day, then each doe has four kits—you're doing the math right— and that happens every third week."

"Sixty-three mice. You're telling me that at minimum I still have sixty-three mice in my house?"

"Not all the same age, of course," she said.

He imagined nightly forays for food, scrabbling in his beloved iron skillets, nibbles out of his soap. Was she pulling his leg? Telling one of her tales? She barely knew anything. "Doe mice?" he asked. "How do you——"

"Whatever. Yeah, sure. Right now they're probably listening to us. They heard everything we did. They probably watched. We probably turned them on," she said.

"So of course quite a few are pregnant," he said. Then he turned to her to see if he'd passed muster.

"Right," she said, smiling, as if he were catching on. "Oh, fun. Done."

He pulled her in close to him, fitted her hips to his. Cozy, warm.

From the kitchen, together, they heard "Snap."

TWINS

Our house is hopping when I get in from Little League. The Hennesseys, Cardulos, people up and down the street are sitting on the porch with no drinks and the dog is going apeshit in the basement. Dad says the Vinales were in an accident. Mrs. Vinales is still under observation, but doing well considering. Mr. Vinales's leg has already been operated on. Vinny, the twin with the missing front tooth, is being "prepared"—Mrs. Hennessey's word—at Spassky's Funeral Home across town. Dad's hand rests heavy on my shoulder when he tells me Bobby, the other twin, is in my bedroom. We're waiting for his uncle from Toledo to take him home. He says Bobby asked to play my drums. I picture busted snares, splintered drumsticks and double-time the stairs.

My door is closed and Mom is singing Bobby "The Little Brown Fox" even though our whole family knows his favorite word is fuck. Saturday nights I babysit the twins. To find out which is which I tickle them. Vinny has the missing front tooth; Bobby's grin is all white and sharp. I dig my fingers into their ribs till they howl.

Bobby is poking my drumsticks into his snotty nose. I sit

at the bottom of the bed where his feet can't reach me. Mom gives me the eye—like I'll know what to say. When she leaves, I tap Bobby's shoes as if I'm playing the drums. We both start to sniffle. I tell him it's okay. I promise him no tickling ever again. I tell him he won't even have to smile.

Everything I Know

My daughter and I both have something to tell each other. So our choice of restaurant was a compromise, and sure enough, our pasta dishes, which on the menu had totally different names, are drowning in identical red sauces. The bread's texture resembles cement dust. But today, food doesn't matter. Finny goes first, age can wait. She says it's about Didier. He is the dour French chef at the four-star restaurant where she has worked on the line for the past two years. Finny pronounces his name *Deed-yay*. As in, I've saved you a piece of *Deed-yay's* lemon tart. She probably has the only Boston fridge with a take-out container filled with homemade chocolate truffles. "*Trouffes*," she says.

"Well, we've decided not to get married," she says. Her straight bangs sway as she talks, freckles everywhere. "Jason probably told you."

Jason is her older brother and she's right; he did tell me. It is something I can count on, one of my three children filling me in on what the other two are doing, who they are seeing, who is thinking of taking a semester off from school, who is growing the discreet garden of marijuana in our Cape house woods. Others might consider it tattling as I once did, but I came to realize they count on not telling me themselves things they think I ought to know. An odd system, but I am the best informed mother around.

"Jason did say something about that," I admit, "about your *not* getting married."

"Good," she says, as if relieved the system hasn't broken down.

Actually, I was hurt she didn't tell me herself. Though I'd heard about the green card issue. Jason is up on this sort of thing because last year he told me that Doug, his younger brother, turned down ten thousand to marry a young Pakistani woman at Berkeley. He was tempted, Finny later added, but he might go into politics someday and it's breaking the law. Lordy, I'd said to her, when did Doug ever consider politics?

"It was Didier's idea to marry," she says, expertly twirling her spaghetti. "The problem is that now I'm sort of in love with him—which ruins everything."

That calls for another glass of wine. "Chianti, OK," the waiter says. Finny nods that she will join me, then informs me that a bad red is always better than a bad white.

"So," I say, "you love him therefore you won't marry him. That's great, where have I been?" I don't say that I was never fond of Didier though his cassoulet could almost make me overlook this.

Eyes glistening, Finny backs up to when it all began, his "Green-Card" proposal that they'd marry so Didier could get his green card. "We weren't in love, so it made things easy: Green card; same mailing address for two years; divorce. Still friends."

I sip my fresh glass of wine because I don't know what to say, and in such situations, whatever I say is usually wrong. These kids have brought me up to know that much. Mom, you don't mean that, they'll say. They're usually right.

"Anyway, marrying Didier for a green card would not have been like being married." Her meal only half finished, she pushes her plate away. I take one more bite and do the same, so as not to offend her culinary sensibilities. "So I've decided not to get married, not because I don't love him, but because now I do. I love a man who does not love me. It would be too much like really being married, do you see?"

Only too clearly, I think. And sadly. But I tone it down and take her hand. "Yes, I think I do see. That's more like what I know." I say this having been through a divorce from her father for something close to this reason.

"Good," she says, and gives my hand a squeeze. We both smile. And now she wants to know my news. It's my turn. Shyly, imagine me shy, I tell her that Arnie and I are getting married. "Fabulous," she says, then, "Have you told the boys?"

I hide a smile in my wine glass. Every time I tell the kids something each wonders if they are the only one to know. Even though I've never told just one of them anything. "I'll tell the boys next week at spring break," I say.

She's happy she's first. "You probably love him," she says.

"I do," I say. Solemnly.

"He probably loves you."

"Probably," I say. I let her have this "probably." She doesn't notice as she clinks my wine glass with hers. "I'm happy for you. I like Arnie. So get married. At your age it's easy," she says.

"No," I say, "it's not easy at any age." When I catch the waiter's eye, she says "I'll get it," as he tallies our bill—no appetizers, no desserts. We know when to abstain.

"No," I say, "I'll get it. Easy, at my age, is picking up the check. But remember there always is one."

"Jesus, Mom," Finny says. "That's what I've been saying. We were there; you taught us everything you know."

PART TWO

WOULDN'T YOU LIKE TO KNOW

Gathered together in her office, we are a mysterious centrifugal force dispersed around the bland interior on two brown chairs and a beige couch. Prior to this session, each of us had a session of our own to discuss our separate malaise. Now, the therapist sits in our circle, in her bland suit, trying for eye contact as if to offer reassurance that she is with us for the long haul.

To be here, my husband needed to inform his secretary to hold this time open, to ask for a continuance on the Haythorpe case, to leave work early and without a bulging briefcase that keeps him in our downstairs study past my bedtime, preparing briefs and citing precedent certainly well past midnight most nights, lights blazing.

To be here, our daughter had to deign to emerge from her bedroom whose canopied bed is now hung with mosquito netting she refuses to discuss, emerge from behind dark glasses, out from under headphones, to deign to join us, arms crossed over a Marilyn Manson t-shirt, one of a wardrobe of thirty mostly on the floor.

To be here, our son was subjected to another fatherly,

lawyerly outburst he no longer finds threatening, although my husband hasn't figured this out yet, so I stepped in to threaten cancellation of the DSL line, and the possible withdrawal of help with college applications scattered around his bedroom where he sleeps in front of the monitor with the lights on.

To be here, I needed to acknowledge a puzzled desperation, to make the appointments, to write my husband a reminder, to watch my daughter write the appointment in black ink on the palm of her hand, to stick a Post-it on my son's new flat screen monitor. I needed to leave the rosewood desk in my study where I write my weekly column on new restaurants, to forego meditation, to leave my book on the guest room bed, where I too frequently sleep and sometimes daydream of the ghost who wanders through the house, long skirts swishing against hard-edged Danish furniture, lantern held yearningly high in her search for something or someone. I needed to demand that the family converge, to entice us to assemble, to cajole us to arrive today at roughly the same time to hear just where we go from here.

But before the therapist tells us where we go from here, she says she has something else to tell us. Then she laughs, a tinkly laugh she surely would have taken back had she realized how utterly dismissive she sounds about the one thing, the only thing she could have said to send us out of her office forever, not cured—cured of what anyway—but a family again.

Giggling, my daughter is the first to rise and announce "that settles that." Her brother follows her out the door asking "was it pearly white?" and then their father stands and looks around as if in this instance precedent had somehow failed him, but he's willing to give it another chance. He follows after the kids, calling "why don't we all go to lunch." The therapist is clearly feeling left out, but what can I do except eventually pay her bill. I join my family in a gust of warmly cold wind, replaying what the therapist said, moments ago, when we were still gathered in her circle, before we became a family again, a family hysterical with complicity and relief. Just after she said, "Before we begin, wouldn't you like to know: you have all seen the ghost."

Numb Enough

He asks again, "Numb enough?" I am tilted back in the dentist's ergonomically correct chair and he is hovering over me, his eyes hopeful above the white mask covering his mouth and nose. Out of sight, he is holding a needle I manage never to see.

Sometimes it takes three shots of Novocain for me to reach the required state of bliss—and I am grateful that he is willing to take me there. I need to be numb enough. Besides, I've had practice—with the death of a husband, the decampment of a lover, the perfidy of children, the betrayal by a best friend, and now the impending demise of my favorite cat. It's not the same but it is.

My previous dentist always insisted I let him try again after one shot, as if I could possibly have faked the sudden, erratic movements of my arms and legs when his drill hit a nerve. "You're only feeling the vibrations of the drill," he'd say. For sure I know the distinction between pain and vibrations, but I'd open wide for another try. And once again, involuntarily, my arm would fly up, or my right foot would lock onto my left knee. He'd look at his watch, and reluc-

PAMELA PAINTER

tantly we'd go for the second or third shot. I decided it was time for a new dentist.

Today, per usual, I tolerate my new dentist's taste in music—at least the annoying, dogged techno beat is as reliable as he is. We're on my third shot.

With my tongue, I probe my back left molar, the source of last night's total lack of sleep. I am numb where I should be numb, so I manage to tell him "num nuff." He is pleased that he can begin to work. "Open wide," he says, and he is in.

AFTER KEY WEST

We're in Key West to heal our marriage following on my husband's recent disclosure. I am somewhat curious as to how the therapist thinks this interlude is going to work. The magic sunsets of Key West? Afternoon margaritas? Yesterday we counted thirty-three six-toed cats at Hemingway's house.

Today, we have come to spend the afternoon at the Maritime Museum—disappointed that it's really only a two-story house on Main Street. Our guide is a little old man with white tufts in his ears and a liver-spotted head. He carefully locked the door behind us after we entered and said it was twenty dollars for the special guided tour. We didn't want the special guided tour, but there seemed no graceful way to say so. My husband shrugs and I giggle. We are caught.

The walls are covered with prints of sailing ships, sea battles, whaling expeditions and he narrates the provenance of each one. I wander away to look at antique compasses in a glass case but his voice reels me back to where he is still expounding on the clipper ship that was the largest of them all. There's something familiar in the guide's headlong rush of words as he tells us about the whaling trade in the

Caribbean seas, something vaguely familiar in the torrent of details about masts and cannons and piracy on the high seas of the 18th and 19th centuries. He doesn't stop or even slow down as he leads us into the next room filled with cases of scrimshaw—whales' teeth or bones with tiny etchings of whale hunts, the great sailing ships, and of course sinuous mermaids with undulating locks of hair—the seaman's fantasy. Our guide's voice intones that this is proof that a sailor's time was not all work and weather, his voice sincerely insincere. And suddenly I know why this is all too familiar: I recall the years when we were remodeling the house, and Jimmy was doing badly in tenth grade, and my operation kept me bedridden for a month. I recall my husband's softly penitent voice telling me of the women behind the days he called to say he's been delayed in Dallas, that the weather in Chicago has grounded all planes, that the meeting in Seattle didn't end well and requires another day of negotiations, that the rental car was stolen and the Portland police need a statement, that the job interview in Cleveland went well, but he's been asked to return tomorrow. It is the same rush of words as our elderly guide at the Maritime Museum, the same level of sincerity.

Now I'm trailing behind our guide who is telling my husband that this particular collection of scrimshaw is one of the world's rarest, with a particularly large display of the scrimshander's tool—needles used to sew sails. I want to ask our guide a question, but I don't know how to interrupt the flow of words. "Stop," I say, "I want to ask . . ." at which our guide swivels around, his gnarled hand steadying himself against this awkward unplanned move. Wringing his hands, he says, "Please, I can't stop, if I stop I'll have to start all over again at the beginning." I tell him "oh please do go on." I don't want to hear it all again.

Stroller

He is waiting on the banks of the Charles River for a stroller to stroll by. A stroller like himself who lacks company, whose pace will not outpace his own, a stroller who might be whistling or humming some silly tune totally out of keeping with what is to follow. Tonight the sliver of moon is turning the choppy water into a silvery pointillist drama. His hands are cold in spite of new leather gloves. He fears the river will freeze within the next few weeks. It is the anniversary of his mother's death.

He was never told the details of his mother's death by drowning when he was almost four. He only knew that he felt an immense watery sorrow, and for years he never asked—he simply made up the entire scene. Or rather pieced it together. He pictured her standing on the bridge where they took daily walks he dreaded over the widest part of the river—he strapped into his stroller so she could move along at a brisk pace. Then along toward the middle of the Longfellow Bridge, she'd lift him out and, in the same fluid movement, up to the green railing to watch the sailboats skim the water. She'd sit him on the railing, his legs dangling out, her arms cozy around his middle, her sharp chin digging into his neck. Her songs were always about the sweet darkness under the surface of the water, and how warm it would be. Lullabies with his name instead of "baby." She'd tell him that maybe, just maybe, she should let him drop. She seemed to consider it forever before lifting him down, flakes of the railing's green paint sticking to his hands. So he never pictured her jumping. It was always a fall, like the fall he would have taken if she'd opened her arms and let him drop. He pictured her bending, balancing over the railing to stare into the river, then lifting first one leg and then the other, sliding over to drop, fall, land, splash, and sink. Something they all do. He hears her behind him still, she seems always behind him, and they always walk away together from their cries, the deep cold splash.

The first stroller was his age, a man in his late forties. He was wearing a blue baseball jacket, blue and shiny with pride, the team's name a hot crescent of red letters on his back.

He no longer imagines his father's fall—what his mother called "his fall from grace." For several years after his mother's death, he supposed that someone named Grace had dropped his father into the river.

His first stroller was strolling along on their bridge. He'd given some thought to the degree of forward momentum required to lift and pivot a stroller as opposed to, say, a jogger. A jogger would be all elbows and knees, too many angles and too much potentially negative energy Strollers on the other hand are relaxed, contemplative, lonely, depressed, limp with sadness, one might almost say ready to die. It is this limpness, a subconscious tilt toward the railing as if they have already thought of it themselves; it is this limpness that he counts on. They help each other.

It was a night like tonight, cold, dark, when he helped

the first stroller out, or rather over. He followed behind that stroller for a while, gauging his own forward momentum to that of the stroller, as if he were pushing him along in a stroller.

He enjoyed the brush of the railing against his sleeve, savored the flow of the railing under his glove. It was dark, or he would clearly have seen the river far below reflecting blue sky instead of the tiny flakes of light from the city's skyline, from the building where he shreds paper five nights a week.

That night he picked up speed. Silent speed. He was bending, sloping over toward the stroller's legs, his shoulder dropping by slow degrees, until he must have looked, to anyone watching, as if he himself were falling, tripping just behind the stroller, except that he'd made sure no one was watching. They were alone, as he dropped and sort of scooped at the stroller's ankles with his gloved hands, the stroller's weight, legs leaning back against his arm for seconds in a startled tilt toward the railing, a dark gray railing used as the pivot point to lift, hoist, push, release, and finally drop him. Over. Down. There was some satisfaction in that.

His mother must have loved him not to let him fall. He told himself this when he was finally told that yes, it was a death by drowning, that she jumped to her death. A certain lack of precision in "jumped"—because he knew she fell. He has been taking care of strollers for two years now. His mother did not return and they do not return either.

Someday soon, when sorrow makes him limp and heavy, when he is unable or unwilling to lift one more stroller, there is only one more he can help. At that time, he will imagine the slight polite lift from behind, the push of concern. He will already feel the wet pull from the other side from years ago, the railing beneath his tiny hands, his legs, when his mother tempted him and was herself tempted, and the last sound he will hear will be a duet with his mother's song.

GOD

My friend calls and tells me there's no other way. She says it's bad news and she'll just come out and say it: "Julia is dead." There are two Julias in our lives, both with a Jake in theirs. My friend is crying. She says Julia was driving to work. . . . I picture one Julia hunched forward in her red Volkswagen, her students' essays on Virginia Woolf scattered in the passenger seat, her breath steaming up the window as she uses a glove to wipe the moisture from the glass. Dogs would be bounding at her door, not happy at being left behind. Her husband would haul them back and slap the fender in farewell before he went back to patching shingles that had blown off the front porch roof. I picture the other Julia throwing files and briefs into her Honda, toast with chunky peanut butter perched next to the scratched-up sunroof. Her mind would already be at the office where she is a public defender, coaxing clients to believe in justice.

My friend says that a delivery van skidded over black ice into Julia's car. They rushed her to the hospital and operated for six hours but she never woke up. Jake is devastated. I picture Julia's pale blond hair dyed red with blood and spread on a white gurney, her clothes cut off, tubes and machines doing their work. Jake, her husband, weeps over her hands. There is no talking to him. Then I picture the other Julia's short black hair slicked wet with blood, her clothes cut off, tubes and machines doing their work. Jake, her brother, weeps above her pillow. His head is bowed in disbelief at this horrific ending to their petty—her words to me in a phone call just last week—estrangement.

I have to ask; there's no other way. I say to my friend, tell me, which one, which Julia? And—like God—she does.

Wyeth Drama: the Missing Scenes

Scene # 1: SUMMER HOME; CUSHING, MAINE. NIGHT

In view of Andrew Wyeth's fading reputation, (which Betsy is too circumspect to mention), she tentatively raises the possibility that the new paintings would sell for more money if there were a little fanfare surrounding their release. Perhaps a mystery? Andrew's ears perk up. They need money. The *Price Guide to Fine Art* lists him at new lows. Besides, art critics have always been wrong about him; he's not rich from the proceeds of poor art; he's poor, damn it, and his art will outlast them all. What did she have in mind? Well, for instance—the Helga paintings. (She is referring to the 246 drawings, watercolors, and paintings of Helga Testorf that Andrew did over the last fifteen years.) Andrew is dense at times. The pictures of Helga? No, Betsy says, *The Helga Paintings. The Helga Series*—does he hear the difference? He does. You mean. . . ? Yes, that's what she means. They will need Helga's help, of course. Andrew always said Helga had the loyalty of a Spaniel (to herself Betsy invariably enlarges the image to include intelligence), so perhaps he could talk to her. Andrew eyes Betsy shrewdly but sees she is only after money, not revenge.

Scene # 2: HELGA'S FARMHOUSE. DAY.

Helga is surprised to see Mr. Wyeth. He has stopped painting her. Perhaps she is getting too old for that sort of thing. He lets her make him a pot of fresh coffee, just like she used to do when she was cooking and cleaning for his sister, Carolyn. Helga, he says, what we had together belongs to the world. My paintings belong to Time. These are Betsy's words, but he doesn't have many of his own. Artists often get by without them. He tells Helga that he is going to sell *The Helga Paintings*. Helga sighs at the sound of her name. Silently, they remember the long hours of her sittings—even though, bored, she slept through many of them. She nods, would he like more coffee. He would. The reporters, he says they're something. They'll hound us. Helga shrugs. She has two Dobermans. She doesn't have to talk to reporters does she? Never. Andrew assures her that Betsy is going to handle everything. Betsy's name makes Helga shy and she stands to pour more coffee. Helga and Betsy have never met, which is just as well.

Scenes # 3, 4 and 5, etc.: SUMMER HOUSE, CUSHING, MAINE. VARIOUS TIMES

Betsy is handling everything. She and Andrew have retitled several paintings. One, a gift to Betsy, is now called *Lovers* at Betsy's suggestion. What could Andrew say? A budding art collector, Leonard E.B. Andrews, who lives in a nearby town, is brought to the Wyeth's mill by a local decorator to view the paintings. (He is a publisher of nineteen newsletters which include the *National Bankruptcy Report* and *Swine Flu Claim and Litigation Reporter*.) He wants the paintings. He makes an offer, rumored to top ten million. Andrew and Betsy keep straight faces until they can blame their glee on their champagne celebration. Mr. Andrews promises to keep the series intact and traveling. He also owns copyrights, but he will not make Helga balloons, although books, calendars, postcards, and posters are in the works. Charlton Heston, out of place in suit and tie, is hired to narrate the video. Andrews says he feels like Ross Perot must have felt when he bought the Magna Carta. He is youngish, eager, and when smiling reminds Andrew of a groundhog he once considered painting against a barn.

The National Gallery of Art announces plans to show *The Helga Series* the following spring. So what if the Met's former curator churlishly complains that Wyeth is "the Williamsburg of American painting—charming, especially when seen from a helicopter." Reporters importune the Wyeths for interviews—thank God. Thomas Hoving, an old friend, can be counted on: he talks. In fact, a *USA Today* headline proclaims "Everybody Talking About Secret Model." As planned, Helga refuses to talk. The only hitch is a son who says, when told his mother is famous, "It doesn't do me any good, does it?" When reporters ask for more, the son belatedly shuts up.

Also as planned, Betsy obliges reporters with interviews. Andrew is too reserved, she tells them. She says *The Helga Series* is his best work. (Only the *Times* refuses to capitalize "Series." But of course that is the newspaper with the wishy-washy critics.) *Art &Antiques* magazine asks Betsy two questions: Why did her husband keep the paintings a secret? And what are they about? Betsy hesitates dramatically, then she says, "love." Yes the Helga paintings are about—love. She tells reporters of the gift Andrew made to her of an early work—the one she retitled "Lovers." She tells how suddenly one day a few years later Andrew told her to go up the stairs into his studio in the Mill to see what he'd been up to for the past fifteen years. (Hoving reports she said "They'd better be good.") And there they were. Betsy is eloquent. Ah, his perceptions, the spirit, the energy—the love.

Although Andrew is gratified by the *Time* and *Newsweek* covers, he soon sheepishly stops reading Betsy's interviews. As for how Helga is taking it? "I just keep away from that," he says. But there is no stopping Betsy. She tells reporters, "He made an interesting remark. He said, 'Of all the things I did of Helga sleeping, I finally resolved it when I did *Night Sleeper*.' And that is a 6-foot by 4-foot painting of a dog sleeping." There is just no stopping Betsy at all.

PAMELA PAINTER

Nose Interview

A few minutes into my job interview, the interviewer passes his index finger swiftly under his nose, which makes me wonder if my own nose possesses an indiscretion, so I surreptitiously pass the index finger of my right hand under my own nose, then casually glance down and am relieved to see nothing untoward, so I answer his next question about my career goals with confidence, only to find it shaken when he rubs his nose again, across then back, which makes me suspect that I failed to find whatever might be there, whatever he might unconsciously be erasing, whatever is probably still lurking there, so I mirror (oh for a mirror!) his gesture—back and forth—just managing to snag the thread of our conversation, something about assessment or test analysis, sniffing discreetly just after he sniffs, as he goes on to ask if I've tested fiberoptic parts before, to which I reply, after also sniffing yet again, reply with a gigantic lie that I've been working with fiberoptics for the past two years, immediately leading me to feel as if I am growing a Pinocchio nose, which brings to mind Freud who said "Everywhere I've been a poet has been there first," before I refocus my attention on the next question in order to conjure up the next big lie, then watch in dismay as the interviewer raises an investigative hand again to pinch the end of his nose, the pads of his thumb and forefinger sort of pressing on the rims of his nostrils as his fingertips move toward the very tip, hiding his nostrils for a millisecond, and (it occurs to me that *nostrils* is an odd word to be looked up later) at the same time I wonder should I attempt the same gesture, and yes, I do attempt it, and you can imagine my relief when a furtive glance at my fingertips confirms that they have come away with nothing to show for the effort, which should be reassuring, till the interviewer sniffs again, twice, before his next question.

ICE

"Jesus, Keaton, how can you expect us to drink here anymore if you don't furnish ice," Roger called from the kitchen. He and the Inspector were peering into Keaton's fridge. Belatedly, Keaton remembered ice.

"Damn trays are frozen in place," the Inspector said. A biochemist, he knew his trays and had the odd habit, for only being twenty-five, of slowly nodding in agreement to most observations. They called him the Inspector. His contribution of tonight's bourbon was sitting on the counter. Sour, smoky vapor from the open fridge was billowing into the room.

"The trays are probably empty anyway," Roger said, his new beard giving authority to his complaint. "Anybody fill the trays last Saturday?"

Keaton knew "anybody" meant Keaton. His friends were pissed and he didn't blame them. It had been a whole five months since Carmel moved out, and Roger and the Inspector started coming over Saturday nights. Their women lived out of town; Roger's was getting a Ph.D. in medieval studies at NYU and the Inspector's lived in Paris. They weren't into bars and Keaton wasn't into the bar scene. They were into ice.

"Let me look," Keaton said. He dumped black pawns onto the chessboard and joined them in the kitchen. His fridge was ancient, with one outside door and a metal freezer section inside with its own little door above the place for keeping things merely cold—the kind you see on porches in rural West Virginia. Edges of the freezer were round and white with frost, and the metal door was three inches from closing.

"Hey, we warned you about ice the last time," the Inspector said, then looked around in further accusation to ask, "Have you been feeding Nietzsche?" When Carmel was clearly gone, the Inspector brought Keaton a white rat from his lab for company. It rustled and squeaked beside Keaton's computer as he wrote software for medical diagnostics—but by Saturday he needed human company. Roger, an architect, had insisted Keaton shift his furniture around to exorcise Carmel's presence—he'd instructed Keaton to slide their bed under the eaves, and the couch in the next room no longer sat snugly in front of the fireplace. It had helped a little, but after a week Keaton put the bed back in its original spot.

"Maybe we should go to my place?" Roger said, tugging on his beard. "Inspector?"

Panicking, Keaton pleaded, "Hey guys, don't leave." He banged the heel of his hand against a buried ice cube tray.

"Well, he looks like he's getting fed." The Inspector had retrieved Nietzsche's cage from Keaton's office and set him next to the chessboard where he chittered away, fat and white.

"Or we could go to your place?" Roger said to the Inspector. "You could rescue Nietzsche?" The Inspector nodded, still inspecting Nietzsche for signs of neglect.

"You guys are jerks," Keaton said.

PAMELA PAINTER

"Who's the jerk," Roger drawled, in his Texas twang.

"Enough," the Inspector said. He gave Nietzshe's cage a pat then returned to the kitchen. "Pull the plug and turn off the fridge."

Roger felt behind the fridge for the plug, his tie hanging down like a plumb line. The fridge died with a clunk.

"There's nothing in here going to spoil that fast," the Inspector said, dismissing cans of tuna fish and sardines, Chinese leftovers in white takeout boxes with little metal handles. "We're going to do a fast defrost." He poked around in the silverware drawer for a butcher knife then began chipping away at the ice around the trays.

Resigned, Roger poured three glasses of bourbon and took a sip. He made a face. "This particular year definitely needs ice."

"I know, I know, I brought it," the Inspector said. He was now wielding the knife like a dagger. "This job needs an ice pick."

"I have an idea," Keaton said. He headed into the bedroom to look in the boxes Carmel said she'd be back for. Her silver hairdryer was in here somewhere. As he fished among her fossil collection, ballet shoes and books, he wondered how she was drying her long thick hair and pictured her sitting between some new guy's knees—then stopped. He would not cry. The dryer was in the second box.

"Carmel's," Keaton said, waving the dryer, and closing the bedroom door so Roger couldn't see that the bed was back in its old place.

"Man, you got to get over that woman." Roger turned Carmel's dryer on to fast and high and directed a hot stream of air into the tiny compartment. Keaton sniffed, remembering Carmel's apple shampoo, the annoying mist on the bathroom mirror.

Solemnly, the Inspector watched things melt, then

sopped up puddles with paper towels. Keaton threw out gravel-gray cheese, a lime hard as stone—jars he didn't have the stomach to open. When he pushed the last of Carmel's chutney to the back of the shelf, the Inspector spied her name and the label's date and insisted on opening it. "You can't throw that out," Keaton said, so the Inspector passed it under his nose, then tossed it into the garbage. Meekly, Keaton found a sponge and began wiping down the shelves.

"Now we're humming," Roger said, the butcher knife in one hand, Carmel's dryer in the other.

Citing bacteria, the Inspector soaped a sponge then set to wiping the stove burners. To show he was trying, Keaton scratched around the kitchen floor with a broom.

Finally, the frost was retreating from the dryer's assault and Roger was able to pull one ice cube tray free. "Empty." Disgusted, he handed it to Keaton and Carmel's dryer to the Inspector. More chunks of frost broke free and Keaton threw them in the sink. Guiltily, he attacked the week's—maybe two week's—stack of dirty dishes. Five minutes later the Inspector turned the dryer to low and announced his arm was tired. He looked at Roger, then Keaton. "Your turn."

"OK. Let's get this over with," Keaton said. With Carmel's dryer back on high, he pointed at the last of the frost and finished it off, a white tide going out. A bit of pressure and two more trays lurched free. Amazingly, one tray actually had six fat cubes in it. Roger plopped them into the glasses of bourbon and made a toast "to ice."

Finally, the freezer door was capable of closing. Like kids, they all tried it. Roger plugged it in and Keaton turned it on. Then he filled the ice trays with cold water.

"Guess we'll stay," Roger said, moving to the chessboard. The Inspector pinged Nietzsche's cage and told him he could stay too.

"You two play," Keaton said, "I'll sit the first one out." As

PAMELA PAINTER

Roger made a move—pawn to king four—Keaton sat back and closed his eyes. He and Nietzsche would settle in and listen to the fridge hum as ice began to form, grateful that water turns to ice.

AIR SHOW

There are twenty of us in the Captain's office, brainstorming new tricks, slick formations for the show. "Attendance is down," the Captain says and we know what's coming. Nervous talk about Medina's fiery crash at the Phoenix fairgrounds last July. His plane peeled off the tightest V formation ever flown and headed straight for the lowest, nearest mountain. They said the crowd's gasp near scorched the grass on the landing field. His crash made page one in every paper but *The New York Times*. My girlfriend tucked the clippings into the back of the album she keeps on me.

"You guys need to really get it on," the Captain says, his chin deep in Air Force medals.

"Hell, we get any tighter," Gates says, "our wings'll be kissing pilots' asses just before we all explode." He is folding paper airplanes that are tight with angry creases and aerodynamic precision. Gates and me, we sometimes sit over a beer and talk about getting out, maybe into commuter runs or civilian cargo. We joke about flying real slow to Peoria or Peru.

"Can't Design give us multicolored exhaust, Walt Disney

colors?" Banko says. And Hennesey, "Let's fly that rock star who looks like Marilyn Monroe." "Or hire all those out-of-work Russian astronauts," Mendez says. The rest of us chime in saying get the President to sing "The Star Spangled Banner," or hey, we could scramble in a snowstorm—if anyone would come.

Gates wings a paper plane at each of us, and finally, after more dumb, desperate suggestions, we wind down.

"Truth is," the Captain says, "I got my orders yesterday. We gotta do what we gotta do." He squares his shoulders as he says this and slaps his cap upside down on his desk, settling everything.

Soon, it's bristling with twenty folded, crisp white slips.

We jostle slowly into line like last time.

Gates is first to take a slip. In slow motion, he unfolds it and takes a look, then protocol, he holds it up for all to see. Nodding, he refolds it fast and better, to make an unmarked plane winging wild with relief and joy. One by one we shuffle forward. Banko waves his slip under the Captain's nose, saying, there ought to be twenty-one slips in the pot. The only time he could get away with such insubordination. Halfway through, it's my turn. I take a slip and slide my thumb in to undo the fold.

I hold it up to show the buck stopped here.

With a shrug I tell Gates everything: that it's too late for me to get out now, that he has to do Peoria for both of us. Because, now, in the few weeks left before we fly El Paso, now it's just me competing with Medina, me thinking up my own last, best show.

Inside Job

The party at the Associate Chair's home was in full swing, which meant that almost every bottle of bourbon and vodka and scotch had been breached, alarmed pets and small children in pjs had been relegated to the stairs, and the music was considered too haphazard to invite accusations. Discretion about the college's most recent search was also being breached, though in euphemisms that Marla declined to follow.

"Better that way, given the litigious nature of academe," her husband would have said had he been standing soberly nearby instead of chatting up the new gaggle of graduate students. One in particular, a rapt dark-haired beauty, was already clearly chosen for his next indiscretion.

Marla herself was still sober enough to realize that she was probably going to cut him loose one of these fine days— or embark on an indiscretion of her own. It made her a bit more attentive (almost for the first time) to her husband's colleague, Jeremy, who often settled near her when a party reached the settling-in stage of guttering candles and lounging, slouching sloth. Her husband was now slouched on the

Victorian loveseat with the young woman whose long hair was so straight she surely ironed it. Oddly, bits were softly attached to her husband's shoulder.

"Water," Marla said, and together she and Jeremy tottered off to the kitchen to look for bottled water. Belatedly, they discovered it was seltzer. Or rather Marla did as seltzer burst forth and drenched the front of her silk shirt. In seconds she was soaked, sopping wet Sodden.

Jeremy unfurled a roll of paper towels and gallantly set about mopping and patting her shirt. "No," she said and took his towel-filled hand. She lifted her shirt and placed his hand here and there. Their eyes met and his hand slowed as he found less and less water. But more of her.

CLEAN

My favorite colleague insists we "drop everything" and have lunch in spite of frantic end-of-semester schedules. When she arrives at my door, the first thing she asks is "are we alone," has anyone happened to hear about our lunch plans? She wants to tell me in person she says, tell me that she's had a persistent, worrying cough and that two days ago her doctor confirmed there is something "suspicious" on the x-rays. We scare ourselves silly by crying.

After she leaves, I pace and pace and finally I vacuum the entire house. I separate out my winter clothes and put them into storage, reduce my summer wardrobe by half. Two days later she calls to say her biopsy is scheduled for the following week. I accompany her to that appointment, neglect the novel in my purse for an article on swans and learn that in Britain, all the swans are owned by the Queen. I see my friend home, whip up a wild mushroom risotto for her to accompany two bottles of an Alsatian white. We talk school politics not worth a fig The next three days I sort photographs, throw out two thirds, and label what is left: family, good friends, bad friends, good vacations, no vacations, conferences, art, pets. I make a "misc" label, then throw all "misc" out. Three days later I clutch her hand as her doctor begins with "I'm afraid I have bad news" and moves on to inoperable lung cancer. Her sleeping pills get us through the night. We settle in to her chemo schedule. Make a list of movies to rent. When I'm not shuttling between her house and mine, I clean the fifty-two drawers in my apartment, beginning in the kitchen. I am surprised by the number of junk drawers (seven) and would not be able to name what each drawer contains if my life depended on it. I regret thinking that thought. My friend loses weight, her hair falls out. I clean her shower drain and later at home I sort through and haul most of the contents of my incorrigible garage off to the swap shop at the town dump. I give away wedding gifts I never opened. And who needs ten sets of sheets. Mornings before I leave for the hospital I go through files and correspondence. She makes a "last will and testament" and asks what I want, she says, "Something to remember me by." I say I don't want her to leave me—or leave me a thing she hasn't given me already. She insists. I resist. Tears. I pet her bald head. Then "the cat," we say in unison; she croaks and I laugh. "Snarky" comes by. Cat food. Cat pillow. After her funeral, still in the cemetery, I can't drive for crying. I pull every manual, registration and gas receipt from my glove compartment, scrape doughnut bags and empty Evian bottles from under the car seats, rip maps from the holders in the doors. I stuff most of it into a crinkly bag from CVS. My address book that night is reduced by half—plus one. The books are next. Snarky has hidden himself in my apartment. He'll turn up or I'll turn him up because I'm not done yet. I am alive. I am clean.

PART THREE

Dud

I've watched it three times and each time I reach the same conclusion: this movie's a dud. It's a dud in spite of the medium-big stars playing network mogul, reporter on the story, mafia patsy, and the TV talking head who spouts the evening's news—the Peter Jennings type. My job's making the trailer. Dark and crowded with expensive equipment, my editing room is plastered with posters of *Casablanca*, *Citizen Kane*, *Unforgiven*—ghosts more alive than the dud running on my screen. Yesterday the boss pulled his glasses down his nose and said over their tops, "Eddie, there's a lot riding on this trailer. No market surveys. We're only doing one."

Today I take a hike down the hall to tell the boss what he must have suspected. For the past two days he's been running through the latest New-Age Western, a movie John Wayne would have shot dead. The boss hits the pause circuit and nods for me to make it fast.

"It's a dud," I say. I tell him I've pieced together ten prelims for the trailer and it's not coming out sweet.

He pulls his tiny glasses to the end of his nose. "Eddie," he says, "who paid you to be a movie critic?" He says with movies a dud is a dud. It's a luxury big directors and rich studios have—making duds—but we don't have that luxury here he says. There's no way the trailer can be a dud.

"Great logic," I say. "The movie's a dud, but the trailer can't be a dud."

He tells me do a preview that will bring the people to the box office before word gets out, before the real critics call it a dud. He pushes his glasses up, already back to work before I've left the screening room.

"Eddie," he says. "Rearrange. Deceive. But if you want to keep your job, don't use the word 'dud.'"

I go back to the editing room where it's waiting like a corpse. What with two sets of alimony and child support payments, keeping my job is top priority, so I need a resurrection. I run the dud through again ready to stop at any even slightly promising moments. I make myself forget the plot. The dud doesn't have a plot. I hit the switch and take it in. It's me and the dud.

I look for sex, action; I look for bodies and blood; I look for weapons.

There's a spot near the end of the movie where they're having a fractious meeting and someone pulls a gun and shoots in order to get everyone's attention. Believe it or not, that's the only role the gun has in the story. I write ll2:34 to ll2:59 to let the cutter know to start with these frames. Then I think: OK I have a gun. Now it's got to go off big. I try to recall any falling bodies, any blood. There's a scene right at the beginning where the talking head slips on a banana peel and ends up flat on his stomach with a bloody nose, a fat lip. I rewind fast. I look for the banana peel. Bingo! I can actually show the fall happening after the gun goes off and there are sixteen seconds where the banana peel does not show. One clip done—a body almost dead from the gun going off. Chekhov would be proud.

Sex. I fast forward to the network mogul's office where he is yelling "No, no, no," into a high-tech laser phone. He's trying to drown out his wife who's called to complain about another fancy dinner party he is going to miss. He looks frantic to get off the phone. His Chinese takeout just arrived and he has a fetish about eating food hot. I write 15:15 to 15:32.

Inspired, I fast forward to the nude scene in the hot tub, where the talking head and the reporter are refreshing themselves after screwing. A phone beside the hot tub is ringing but they ignore it. I do not. I reverse the order and feed forty seconds of hot tub, wet flesh and ringing phone into ten seconds of the mogul screaming "no" into another phone. Who says they have to be the same call. I'm feeling lucky about this dud.

Next I remember a low-key chase scene in the shopping mall where the reporter is hysterically hunting for the right trench coat for her first big story. I splice it together with the Mafia patsy's shakedown of a liquor store in a seedy part of town. I relocate the liquor store in the mall. So it's a slight change of neighborhood, but hey. Time flies as I make notes of where to cut and splice, cut and splice.

When I finish, it's a winner. My dud has a new story. My dud almost cons me into thinking the movie's worth seeing.

Why did I think this would be so hard?

Who says the story you tell has to be the story that happened?

Cut and splice. It's what I do every night warming a bar stool at O'Toole's: exaggerate, lie, edit. Hey Eddie, someone will say and then I'm off on another story before I head for home. It's what I do most nights when I can't sleep. It's what I do with my life.

What I See

Those sinewy lines are real. I am standing on the edge of a friend's blue tile swimming pool and just this instant I realize that those lines I saw and was amused by in a David Hockney painting are the real thing. I turn to call to my wife but she is deep in conversation with Max who is generously mixing her one of his slushy margaritas. His wife is sunbathing, against all reason, her eyes closed. I turn back to those yellow wavy lines in my friend's pool. I am seeing them for the first time. Hockney has made me see something I discounted in his paintings as an artist's license to paint anything. Even silly lines. These lines must be ridges reflecting the Cape summer sun—lines most apparent in Hockney's painting *Peter Getting out of Nick's Pool*. Sinewy lines made up of thin reeds of red and orange, and before this moment totally unbelievable.

At the MFA exhibit, I marveled at the nerve of Hockney to paint those lines, when his rendering of Peter's naked back as he perhaps contemplates getting out of the pool is so marvelously real. His hands flat on the hot concrete surrounding the pool. His wide shoulders hunched around his neck, his head turned to the right, his mouth hidden by his raised right shoulder. Strong shoulders taper to a waist, then the slight flare of hips made for holding on to, when what I thought of as imaginary lines approach his bare buttocks. His cleft is a rich sienna or raw umber slash with one wavery, solid watery line in particular moving through his slightly parted legs—a line that surely ends somewhere. Peter is looking off to the right—he doesn't seem to be getting out of the pool. Perhaps he is looking for Nick. Perhaps he is waiting for an invitation. Perhaps the tension in his arms is the real invitation.

Hockney has made me see. I look around my friend's pool to see what else I see. I see hummingbirds with invisible wings, crimson trumpet vines eclipsing whatever structure lies beneath its canopy, becoming the more solid of the two. I see my wife deep in conversation with my best friend, Max—her gaze locked on his, their drinks held in silent salutation, an invisible filament between them as tangible, as breakable now, as glass.

NOT A GHOST STORY

If this were a ghost story, I could tell you about songs whispered into my voicemail, "for you, Mona;" footsteps outside my dorm room at 3 a.m.; bottle caps arranged like coins across the hallway from my door.

If this were a real ghost story, I'd tell you how the elevator always rises to the seventh floor; how it opens to a stench I remember from last semester's chem lab; and going down how it bypasses first and drops to the fluorescent basement maze. I'd show you how postcards and letters in my mailbox arrive wrinkled and slightly damp; I'd pull out essays returned with words crossed out like "pantomime," "acquiesce," and "love;" books with torn-out pages and magazines with all the coupons filled in. I'd describe the bored disbelief of my dorm advisor who has faith only in the guy supplying her with drugs.

In a ghost story, graffiti would be taken seriously and photographed, the janitor wouldn't dare scrub it away with a shrug; bloody handprints on the bathroom walls would make sense; underwear wouldn't just reappear.

In a ghost story, the living characters would confront

the dead, naming names, revealing motives; instead of narrowing to infinity, the plot would thicken; time would never stand so still.

If this were a ghost story, I could turn my flashlight on and read under the covers late into the night. I could hold my breath. I could turn to the last page to find out what happens. If this were a ghost story, I could count on knowing it would end.

First Night Of Married Life

He said I can't believe it's really over? *She* said were we required to stay to the end? *He* said did you see your Aunt Harriet take off with two of the rose centerpieces before the reception was finished. *She* said I thought your father was supposed to pick up the liquor tab. *He* said no, only the rehearsal dinner. *She* said I didn't know it was just going to be appetizers followed by appetizers though there was lots of wine. *He* said I think your cousin-the-chef nabbed the leftover cases of Burgundy. *She* said Bordeaux. It's probably on the restaurant's video cam. *He* said if your mother hadn't picked a dickhead society photographer he wouldn't have been stranded in Venice. *She* said your sister repeatedly assured us that her adorable three-year-old ringbearer would not drop our wedding rings. *He* said I told you it should have been a child-free wedding. *She* said we forgot family-free. *He* said it was my family that was outnumbered. *She* said your mother's neckline was much too low as the mother of the groom. *He* said out of bounds. *She* said really! *He* said your mother had her fingers all over the wedding. *She* said at least one hand was writing out checks. Well I would have chosen a different best man if I'd known your brother would get a Mohawk two days before the wedding. *She* said wasn't your cousin supposed to be in charge of transportation for the out-of-town, out-of-country guests? Get them places on time. *He* said how could my cousin know that the patriarch of your family had somehow gotten himself locked in the bathroom? *She* said which friend recommended that awful band? *He* said your maiden aunt evidently needed to, as they say, cut loose, and the band probably helped. *She* said "cut loose" with your gigolo uncle. *He* said how did we end up with, with—you know, those flowers they always have at funerals. *She* said you mean the chrysanthemums your mother's florist sent as a gift. *He* said what are we going to do with all the Tiffany vases. *She* said they are more useful than the Scottish coat of arms from your fraternity brothers. Especially since I'm keeping my maiden name. *He* said we'll have a garage for the coat of arms. *She* said and the Tiffany vases. *He* said . . . never mind. *She* said right, we can take it all back.

Driver's Test

We are in the slow lane traveling west on the Pennsylvania Turnpike. We're moving West *and starting over*—my husband's words. He is driving as if his mind is already somewhere else; I'm collecting skid marks.

We were still talking to each other when we started out from Baltimore, when I first wondered out loud what story lay behind a startling set of black curved tracks before us on the road.

"Don't think about it," he said. It is something he's said too many times before: about our lost calico in grad school, my grandmother's singed quilt, Molly's red tricycle he insisted I give to the abashedly grateful neighbor on the next street.

So I didn't think about it—out loud. I left him to his driving and I allowed myself to imagine what made some car or pickup jam on its brakes hard enough to lay those black satin ribbons on this road. They had unravelled for over fifty feet, a desperate curve whipping twice across the line dividing two lanes on this divided four-lane interstate until they stopped abruptly. What made them stop? Did the brakes work, do their job, stop 2,000 pounds of glass and metal as they were supposed to? The car halting just short of an uninterested bull moose ambling across the pavement in search of marshy grass, or just short of some other disaster? Perhaps one vehicle met another, say the wall of a semi whose driver had been too long on the road, or the wandering sedan of some solitary person momentarily asleep at the wheel?

Now we're in Pennsylvania, dangerously drifting along the country's first superhighway built when fast meant fifty miles per hour. Our Honda is packed tight with my dissertation books, necessary clothes in duffles, and my husband's hard drives, computers, monitors—all the expensive electronics of a man in touch with the world. The white CorningWare casserole and transparent glass lid we almost left behind are rattling on top of boxes in the back seat, clattering softly in their Corning way—a sound that could never be mistaken for any other.

Starting over. We're *fleeing* to a place where Molly never lived. A place where we'll have to apply for new licenses, be photographed in faces we no longer recognize, retake our driver's test. Learn some other state's permitted speeds, turn-right-on-red rule, animal hazards—their Rules of the Road.

Maybe skidding should be part of the test.

Skidding should be required so you're ready for it—if and when it happens, so you'll know what it feels like when front wheels lock, when you are careening sideways down the road, so you'll know how the only thing you're in control of is the futile pressure of your right foot on the puny, helpless brake. That way, the first time you are told to hit the brakes, the first time you *hit those brakes* with the full desire and intent to stop, stopping doesn't matter. The bored instructor could make a game of saying *now*, somewhere safe in a mowed abandoned field or an empty parking lot so large that contact with anything else is out of the question.

When I break the silence to explain this new test to my husband, my voice is animated for the first time in eight months and catches even me by surprise.

As I describe the test, he turns to me, and his wide profile thins to sharp cheekbones and angry gray eyes. When I tell him *imagine your foot hard on the brake*, when I say *please, just try*, he fails.

At the next rest stop, I wait till he has disappeared into the Men's and then I gather up the Corning casserole and its offending, murmuring lid and abandon it on a distant picnic table. As we pull out, its blue-white glow grows fainter in the dark.

Once again, we are bored by the landscape of Ohio's I-80 because it is the Ohio we remember from grad school, and once again, we are surprised and then dismayed by Indiana— the state, inspite of maps, we always forgot—somehow expecting to leave Toledo and an hour later find ourselves on Chicago's South Side.

The sun is going down in Indiana when my husband lets me drive. He doesn't want to, but he's tired so he questions me intently. "We could find a place for the night," he says, solicitously, but without looking at me, rubbing his eyes. "We don't have to keep on. Though it would be nice to get in two or three more hours."

"I'll drive," I say. Finally we pull over to exchange places. We don't touch as we pass behind the car—we could be strangers in a used car lot.

Our doors slam shut and I hitch the seat up, adjust mirrors automatically, even though I've rarely driven since the accident, the word accident so inadequate for the amount of loss. The drama of medics, sirens, glass and blood. And skid marks.

I am a collector now.

The next skid marks are short and conjure up a scurrying profligate animal who safely braved these lanes. Another set of marks is so precisely there that surely measurements of length and gradients and curve were carefully taken and had their day in court. Oddly, the next skid marks almost meander to the shoulder before they shoot straight up a steep bank, gouging out dark dirt lanes where a car must have finally stopped, its driver sweating, shaken at what she'd felt the car do without her. Something she'd never forget even sober, and thank God no one was hurt. This time.

When I glance over at my husband, his head is already bobbing above his rhythmic chest. He's not afraid of sleep, or dreams.

I practice, applying pressure to the gas pedal till we are going 85, then 90, then stepping on the brakes to slow us gradually back down.

When it happens he feels it.

He wakes up as I am laying down our own black silk path of rubber. We're sliding sideways then straight, there are no other lights on the highway.

"What happened, what?" he whispers, sensing that to cry *stop* would be foolhardy. He isn't sure there wasn't a disaster I just avoided as he peers behind us in the night.

Bracing himself—himself—on the dash, he turns to me. "Please, if it's about Molly," he says, please he's ready to talk. But he's too late. Oh we'll survive this skid, but not much else. He's left his marks and now I'm leaving mine.

ARTIST AS GUEST IN THE HAMPTONS

First of all, his wife informed him, we can't possibly have the Horstels to dinner with the Jimm Smythhs because the long dining room wall—the only space large enough for the 6' by 15' paintings they each gave us—is occupied, so to speak. Hanging there is that sixty pound oil and gouache titled *Whale and Water* that Xu Xui announced was her "house gift" in the thank you note she sent express mail a month after her three-week stay. Remember, since she used real glass, *Whale and Water* was too heavy when we tried to lug it down to the basement.

He remembered all too well. Besides, he was still feeling the aftereffects of last fall's hernia from carrying the Lindstrom bronze porpoise from the potting shed to the patio when Sven Lindsrom mentioned he was coming to visit them in the Hamptons to reinvigorate his artistic vision. And no doubt acquire another muse, his wife said. So in addition to having the Horstels and Smythhs separately to dinner, we'll have to wait till our roaming son Charlie is home from his RISD internship to unseat the Xu Xui and haul either the Horstel or Smythh up from the basement, depending on the

PAMELA PAINTER

guest list, to the "place of honor" in the dining room. There the artist was always circumspectly seated across from his or her work, which occasionally had a stultifying effect on conversation, but could also lead to some interesting anecdotes, like the story Tioni used to tell about his painted wooden leg's adventures in Italy before he died. Lord knows where in the garage Tioni's *Afternoon of the Fun* is buried.

Meanwhile, his wife said, about tomorrow's dinner party: the small, lush Klayton watercolor—let's see, that was his house gift four years ago—should probably be moved from the guest bathroom to the entrance way, though it does match the new marble tiles perfectly, and goodness, we can't forget to bring his wife's multicolored, jelly bean platter down from the attic, though we still aren't sure Janine didn't mean it as a joke. And we must call the art restorer to see if he's replaced the matting on the Binner, since they're good friends of the Horstels, and we must also ask if he was able to disinfect the canvas so there is no hint of Nero's recurring bladder problem; it proved so ruinous to the Mendoza triptych that we can only dine out with them, and of course pick up the check year after year after year.

And by the way, his wife said, the Hampton Art Museum called to remind us that we still haven't retrieved the Missy Massey painting that we'd donated to their auction last year. We told her we were donating it, so heaven forbid she asks what it went for. The director suggested that requiring the opening bid begin at $200 might have been a bit high. Surely, her husband said wistfully, someone might be at this year's art auction who really loves Peoria, as in "I 'heart' Peoria," since the Finleys have stopped speaking to us ever since Finn found his "I 'heart' Frogs" behind the ficus in the library. Or was it in the closet?

What is this anyway, his wife said, why can't our artist friends arrive with two exquisite ripe cheeses? Or, he said, a vintage Bordeaux or a good bottle of champagne—house gifts, they agreed, that would disappear at evening's end into the Hamptons' own starry night.

Put To Sleep

Jackson's father calls at 5 a.m. "I'm depressed," he tells Jackson, "but that's not why I'm calling." Jackson's father, who turned ninety-two a month ago, says he just wants Jackson to know he's going to put Bucknell to sleep.

"Dad, you can't do that. Bucknell is a great dog," Jackson says. Bucknell, an Irish Setter who has been a lifeline for Jackson's parents for the past eight years, was named for the college whose football team Jackson's father's team could never beat. Jackson takes the phone from the bedroom, where his wife is sleeping soundly, to his drafting table in the next room. "What does Mom say?"

"She says she won't have to worry about me out walking Bucknell on ice, or keeping track of dog food. Sending Gus out to find those special real meat dog bones." Jackson's mother stopped driving a year ago when she turned eighty. Now Gus shows up twice a week to drive Jackson's parents on errands—the dentist, the doctor, and butcher shop for Bucknell's bones.

"Bucknell's not sick, is he?" Jackson says. He pictures Bucknell drooping over the foot of his parents' bed, snoring noisily through dreams of hunting swift wild animals he's never seen, while Jackson's father is plotting to murder Bucknell. "Give Bucknell to Gus," Jackson says.

When his father counters with "Gus has us," Jackson says, "I'm coming to get Bucknell. I'm bringing Bucknell back home with me. Then we'll talk about depression."

"Nothing to talk about. Depression's depression." His father hangs up.

It isn't light yet when Jackson pulls into his parents' drive. Bucknell's stuff is on the porch, ready to go, in two plastic bags. Jackson's mother is watching Bucknell lope around the dewy yard. She wrings her hands in front of her herbal apron, her eyes are red, but the story has been that Bucknell is his father's dog. Dry-eyed and resolute, Jackson's father appears and makes a gesture that could be hello or goodbye. He doesn't acknowledge Bucknell who is prancing around, pushing a slobbery tennis ball into his crotch.

Jackson loads up the car. When he calls Bucknell's name, the setter bounds down the walk with his breed's reckless stupidity and sits in the passenger seat, happy for the unexpected ride. His wet nose makes a prism of the window. He barks at anything that moves.

Back home, as the sun begins to rise, Jackson puts Bucknell's plaid blanket in the living room near the unused fireplace, his dog dish in the kitchen, his water bowl beside it. Puzzled, Bucknell pads around behind Jackson sniffing as he goes. Jackson tells him everything will be all right. Jackson doesn't know what to tell his wife, who is still asleep. She sleeps through everything.

An hour later over breakfast his wife voices her displeasure with the unexpected guest. Hearing his name, Bucknell thumps his tail. He hovers carefully at a distance, well-trained not to beg at the table. Jackson tells his wife about the new depths to which his father's depression has sunk.

"I'd be depressed at ninety-two," she says, his wife, the psychiatrist.

"I don't find that medically helpful," Jackson says.

"Well, we do seem to have a dog now," she says. She's already dressed for the day, her long hair pulled back from a wise, high forehead and coiled into a bun.

Jackson leaves with Bucknell to buy fat fake bones and a few meaty real ones. They are meant to keep Bucknell occupied while, in the office adjoining the library, his wife sees her patients. She tells Jackson there are personal details that patients shouldn't ever know. They might be freaked out if they heard a dog bark, or even knew they had a dog, never mind a child or children, which Jackson fears they will never get around to planning. "Freaked out" are Jackson's words. "Interrupted transference" are hers.

"The world has dogs in it," Jackson tells her. "The world is full of children and dogs." She doesn't answer. In her world, dogs do not bark.

All day Bucknell obligingly lounges by Jackson's drafting table as he sketches dazzling new kitchens, designs cunning granite countertop arrangements for upwardly mobile tract-home McMansions. While he and Bucknell take long walks in the burgeoning woods across the street, he tells Bucknell about the importance a well-designed kitchen plays in the family dynamic. Bucknell makes proper use of these walks, stopping at trees and fire hydrants, staking out new territory of his own. That night, Bucknell jumps onto the bed, clearly intending to sleep with them.

"Not on the bed," Jackson's wife says, tying her silk pajama bottoms with a double knot.

So Bucknell lurks around the edges of their king-size mattress, a solid alert presence. At 5 a.m. still on Jackson's father's schedule, the dog starts to pace around and sniff. Even with his eyes closed, Jackson feels Bucknell watching them sleep, feels the breeze from his wagging tail.

It's been three weeks. Bucknell now wakes at 6 a.m. He and Jackson watch Jackson's wife sleep. Her hand is tucked beneath a freckled cheek, partially covered with fine, long hair. Jackson smoothes it back and tucks it behind her ear. She opens one eye. Bucknell senses their movements and quickens his pacing. From her side of the bed Jackson's wife says, "Somehow, it's like having your parents in the room. Patrolling our sleep, curtailing our sex life." And Jackson thinks, if it's the dog, *enough of that*.

The next day, Jackson goes over to talk to his father about his depression. They sit around the red and chrome kitchen table, bought in the forties. Jackson's father is wearing a tie with his sweater. Jackson's mother sets the kettle to boiling. "Look at your dad moping around. He misses the dog," she says.

"Dad was depressed *before* I took the dog," Jackson reminds her. "He was going to put Bucknell to sleep."

"Your mother doesn't believe in depression," his father says. "Tell that to your wife."

"You miss Bucknell," Jackson's mother says to his father—her tone accusatory. Jackson's cue.

"Look, I can bring Bucknell back," he says.

"I told you I'll have him put to sleep," his father says. "I'm too depressed to have a dog." His bald head glows in spite of his depression.

Jackson schedules an appointment with his father's doctor who puts his father through a variety of tests. They wait for the results and Bucknell goes through a lot of bones. He now sleeps on the bed with Jackson and his wife, snuffles through satisfying predatory dreams, still wakes too early. "Tell me about the dog," Jackson says to his wife one evening before she turns off the light on her side of the bed.

"It would probably take six months of sessions to unravel the dog," she says into her pillow.

"Bucknell's only eight, so we must have four or five dog years ahead of us to do it," Jackson tells her. Then it occurs to him to ask: "Sessions for whom?" But his wife is already asleep. Bucknell's tail vibrates on the mattress like a drumstick.

Electrolyte imbalance is what the doctor tells Jackson's father. "Your depression is easy to fix. Two miracle drugs will do it." A week later Jackson's father calls again at 5 a.m. As Jackson shuffles into his study, Bucknell jumps down from the bed to follow. Jackson's wife probably thinks the slight movement is Jackson. In a booming voice, his father says he's coming by for Bucknell.

"To do what?" Jackson asks, but his father hangs up. Jackson waits in the kitchen with a wide-awake Bucknell.

"I'm taking him home," Jackson's father says through the screen door, as if he had never threatened any dire alternative. Bucknell lopes around his flannel knees in ecstasy. "Gus is going to stop by PETCO and fill the trunk with dog food," Jackson's father says. He scratches Bucknell's ears in a way Jackson never thought to.

"Aren't you glad I took Bucknell in," Jackson says, handing over Bucknell's blanket, dog bones, leash, dish, and water bowl. Gus waves from the car.

Jackson is to get no credit from his father. "You two ought to get a dog," his father says as Bucknell tugs him down the walk.

"You know we don't want a dog," Jackson says.

His father shakes his head in disgust. "That wife of yours coddles her patients too much. Treats them like kids. You ought to have some kids." Bucknell barks as they all drive off.

What Jackson doesn't know yet is that a year later when his father calls at 5 a.m. Bucknell will already have been put down. His father will have told his mother he was taking Bucknell to Jackson but instead instructed Gus to take them to the pound. "Doing the hard job," his father will say.

There are things Jackson does know. It is still early. Jackson's wife is still sleeping and the newspaper hasn't come. Jackson can avoid patients and designing kitchens for a few more hours. Dogless, he goes back to bed, turns his pillow over, and pulls up the quilt. His wife slumbers on beneath the light touch of his hand on her back. Jackson puts himself to sleep.

Brunch in Black

The table was all wrong. It was too narrow, too long, with a chair at the head, but not—because the table was so long—at the foot. It would feel like a meeting. My daughter and I were being shown to our table in the formal dining room of Boston's Museum of Fine Arts. We were waiting for five others to arrive. And I was waiting for the results of medical tests from three days ago. Sundays are for brunch.

I turned to the hostess to say that my party of seven would much prefer that perfectly round table over there.

"Oh, that table is reserved," she said, not even glancing that way as she placed menus at each place setting of the long table. Unhappily I sat. Minutes went by before we were able to summon a waiter from the wings to tell him that we would indeed like to order a Bloody Mary or perhaps a glass of very cold champagne.

It was then that the hostess swished by and removed my white napkin from its roost on my plate and replaced it with a black one.

I'd never seen a black napkin before, but it did not feel good, that rolled tube of black, a black diploma in front of me.

I studied the dining room as our drinks arrived, but there was no other black napkin in sight. My daughter was puzzled too, but not upset. I was upset. When one is waiting for "news" everything feels portentous, as portentous as a black napkin among all the white ones. Suddenly, I felt this was a sign, perhaps a signal to the waiter that here was a difficult patron. Or a sign for me that all was not well. It was intolerable.

So I rose and walked over to the round table that we were not allowed to occupy and I retrieved a perfectly pure white napkin and in its place I abandoned my black one, harbinger of who knew what. But the damage was done.

My daughter, watching me, had sensed that something was wrong. She had been amused, but was now aware of my immense discomfort. We were both watching the black napkin on the white lake of the round table.

Sure enough, a minute later, a waiter swooped down and replaced it with a white. I had tears in my eyes. A white napkin to wipe them away.

Herself a demanding patron and former restaurant owner, my daughter signaled for the hostess to approach our table and rose to meet her halfway.

"Tell me," my daughter said, pleasantly. "We were wondering what the black napkin is for?" Pleasantly too, the hostess explained that when someone was wearing black, the white napkin was exchanged for a black one. "So there would be no residue of white lint on one's black skirt." On my black skirt. A reprieve, though there are far worse things in the world than lint on a black skirt, and a week later I would learn that I had yet another reprieve. But that day, we dined well, though I would happily have dined on white lint.

PAMELA PAINTER

THE POET

It is true what she says, this gringo poet. She was a guest in my house. My wife who prepared the coffee, my daughter of the manicured nails, my absent son, they remember her. She was all ears. Of course a Colonel must read the papers, keep dogs, have a pistol beside him at all times. But the moon was just the moon. The cop show was in English—people died, the cops won. I'm a cop and if the cops don't win what will happen to this world. Grates on the windows, broken bottles embedded in my walls are a lot less money and trouble than her fancy alarm systems that require reliable electricity or someone to be alarmed and summoned, and all of what that network depends on is her country's history of blood. We fed her. The maid cooked rack of lamb rare, halved green mangoes, uncorked a good wine. I asked the poet how she enjoyed the country. She said nothing memorable so I talked of how difficult it had become to govern. I told her she was fortunate to live in a place with no violence, where the streets are safe as daylight, where the only concern is for human rights. The parrot on the terrace squawked—every parrot talks too much. I saw her friend's warning to say nothing, and I knew this guy would also do nothing. I knew what she wanted—and I wanted her to see what I've been up against. So I brought out my sack of human ears. How does she know they are like dried peach halves? When I shook one in front of her nose she looked away and the one I dropped in water did not come alive. It stayed as dead as the guerrillero who once wore it. Sure I said "tell your people they can go fuck themselves." They have no idea. That is what I believe. All this is true: it was what she wanted to hear. The parrot silenced by my voice, ears swept to the floor, the last of the wine suspended in air. If I go to her house will she be as complete a hostess, will she tell me the secret of her worst deed, will she feed me and let me go out into the world with my pen ready to write—like a gun—only more deadly. She came here greedy, nose pressed to the floor, sniffing around for a poem.

Never Before

Something was very wrong, the ambulance pulsing in place, two EMTs administering oxygen to my husband, reading his blood pressure, doing everything necessary to get him to the hospital alive, all of us waiting for the driver to emerge— from where, where—from inside my house as outside we waited for our desperate ride to Dana Farber, lights blipping, sirens blaring, because minutes earlier I'd tried to wake my husband when he didn't respond to the morning sounds of my stretching, gargling, dressing, of grinding "any coffee beans but Starbucks," and at that point I'd called his doctor who advised me inexplicably "to wait an hour and see if he wakes on his own," wanting to spare me, I'm now convinced, to spare my husband the hospital death scene it became, but after stroking my husband's cheek harder, harder, lifting his shoulders, I called the ambulance because to wait made no sense, and minutes later three EMTs arrived and I ran to throw the door open, stretcher-wide, to lead them to our bedroom where my husband lay, still sleeping, breathing, breathing thready breaths, still not able to wake on his own, wake to his name, to my desperation, a desperation he always found amusing, always mocked, when it had to do with my lost keys, which got lost at least once a day, somewhere in the house, somewhere I had put them down, causing my husband to buy me a key-finder, this gadget he attached to my keys that beeps when one claps correctly, the beep beep cleverly revealing their hiding place, though "correctly" required a loud, palm-filled hollow sound, a clap I never mastered though I practiced, a clap my husband performed like thunder, but that day I wasn't thinking keys, I was willing my husband to wake as the EMTs lifted him onto a stretcher and carried him, twenty-four pounds lighter than two months ago, down the stairs and into the waiting ambulance, back doors winged open to receive him, and in front, the passenger seat high, requiring me to hitch up and on instructions buckle up, and wait, wait for the EMT who was the driver to come gallumphing down the stairs, across the sidewalk, to my door—not the driver's door—but *my* door, his face sweating, desperate, to tell me "never before has this happened," never before has he lost his keys in somebody's house, assuring me he'd called in and another ambulance had been dispatched, its arrival imminent, promising the transfer would be smooth, easy, his eyes pleading, his voice faltering as he said again and again, "never before . . . " and I stopped listening, eyes closed, my own keys in my fist, listening now only to my husband's sounds behind me, knowing that sometime in the future, after the dying, the death, the loss, I would hear the EMT's words telling me something I already knew, as never before.

PAMELA PAINTER

My Honey

For the second time he calls me honey, this famous author, our dinner guest. My husband does not or pretends not to notice. My cousin's eyes widen but she continues to smile. We became acquainted with this famous author after my husband wrote a favorable review of his recent controversial book on another famous author, earning his gratitude and the suggestion that he come to dine. Now, seated nearest him, I pour more Graves into his glass, watering his legendary love for the grape. We will need another bottle for sure. To his dwindling credit he brought two superb bottles of Graves—though he clearly intended them to be shared with him this very evening. I loathe the word "shared." Lately, my eighteen-year-old daughter has been sharing too many of her strong opinions with me. Tonight's opinion was just how late she could stay out with my car. She says it's her freckles that keep me thinking that she's a child.

It is a good Graves. When he gestures with his glass to mine, and says, "Honey, do see to your own lovely self," I forgive him.

Talk has circled around to unsuspecting authors' waning

reputations and their latest recycled books. He assures me that he intends to read mine. When he calls me honey for the fourth time, I put both hands flat on the table, a gesture my husband, for some reason, finds enormously sensual, and I lean forward toward our guest. "Please," I say politely. "Please do not call me honey."

My husband appreciates my gesture, knowing he's the only one who views it that way, and there's no doubt that later tonight we'll make love. He does not, however, appreciate the request I just made to our famous author. My husband clears his throat as our guest rolls right over what I said, as if I, too, merely cleared my throat. More wine slides down, and soon my husband suggests we move to the living room with glasses and sit by the fire to counter the chill in the air.

There is where the famous author calls me honey once again. At this point I drop the famous from my thinking.

Perhaps if I'd been seated across the room, or petting a cat on my lap, or stirring up the fire—anything but sitting next to this man—I would not have thrown my glass of wine at him. Thrown is not quite accurate, it just sounds more dramatic—but what I did was lift my glass, gracefully turn my wrist, and douse his head with his very good Graves.

Douse. He is very wet.

Everyone but me goes into action. The author sits up straight, blinks. Droplets fly. My cousin appears with a pink towel. My husband appears with the famous author's jacket.

They are all talking at once. "Goddamn . . ." the author murmurs from behind the towel. My cousin announces that she is going to make a pot of strong coffee My husband, holding out the author's jacket, apologizes profusely for my bad behavior and says he imagines that the author would indeed like to take his leave.

The author shakes his head, his hair still weeping wine, and looking thoughtfully at me, he says, "No, I'll have a double scotch."

Can the evening move on from here? Well, somehow it does and my daughter is only an hour late with the car. She's read the famous author's books and joins us in the living room where she introduces herself and her freckles, and sits across from us on the Parsons bench. Her jeans have holes at the knees. Clearly she suspects I won't make a scene about her late arrival in front of everyone and she is right. One scene per evening is what I allow myself.

Now the famous author is famous again because my daughter thinks he is. He is also enjoying his double scotch as he asks her about the guitar case she arrived with, college applications and her favorite authors. He is openly gratified that she has read his book, and then I hear it. My cousin hears it. My husband hears it. My daughter hears it too. That "Honey."

My daughter leans forward, arms on her knees, and says, "Whoa. Wait a minute. Did you just call me "honey?"

The famous author laughs. "Of course not," he lies. "Heaven forbid."

We let him lie. That daughter of mine sits back, arms crossed, and smiles. That daughter of mine with her strong opinions, her tantrums and her tears, she has real power. That daughter of mine can do anything she wants.

Touchdown

People don't give other people enough credit. Take me—a paraplegic living with three cats in a first floor apartment with a special van parked at the end of a hardwood ramp. I wrote off all that mushy love stuff ages ago—except for my cats nuzzling around, sleeping on my chest, warming my lap.

I didn't give women enough credit.

Ten years ago I was the best quarterback the high school ever had before some drunken asshole from two towns over ignored the only light on Main Street. Fire department had to use the Jaws of Life to lift his car off mine. When my girl went to Penn State on scholarship, I was still in the hospital starting therapy. The night before she left, two of the guys kept the nurses occupied while I showed her the fancy angles of a hospital bed. It was almost like old times when we used to neck on her front porch swing. Her letters were sealed with red lipstick kisses. They stopped coming near the end of her freshman year—I'd figured it to happen sooner than that. Then I heard she married some guy owns a trailer park on the Florida panhandle.

When I moved into my own place, the cheerleaders

PAMELA PAINTER

took turns bringing over casseroles their moms made. They sewed a slew of curtains and had a painting party that took more time cleaning up. One by one they all got married too. By then they'd turned shy remembering what I once was— the school hero dodging down the field, cradling a football, winning State with two touchdowns; then seeing me like I am now—the wheelchair, legs as thin as their wrists, arms wrapped around a tabby cat. Those girls were looking at the past. I think that's why I didn't count on any woman being able to picture me in her future.

All this is not to say I didn't have a life.

Guys from the old team came by once a week for poker. They wheeled me fishing, got me ringside seats at all the games. Kozak, he built a special ramp to his hardware store where I buy supplies for the toys I carve. But it was true that pretty soon there weren't any women around except the wives. So for years I didn't give women enough credit—credit for plain old curiosity. Which is how it all started.

The first time—with Lorene—was pure accident. Truth is Lorene was mad as hell at her husband the night she went to bed with me. But just being mad wouldn't have sent her down the hall to my door, snuffling and wet-eyed and needing to be held. It was curiosity too and I almost missed it: her wanting me.

The night it happened, she stood outside my door, calling my name: "Cady. Cady, you up?" I was putting a last coat of black semi-gloss on a dozen steam engines, kids need to see what a real train once looked like, imagine the smoke trailing after as it heads into a dark tunnel.

When I opened the door, she hesitated as if to see if she'd gotten me out of bed and a sound sleep. Then she must have smelled the wet paint because she headed straight for the kitchen where most people sit while I carve or paint trains, trucks, houses with roofs that lift off, doll cribs, perfectly balanced tops. I make toys for adults though I disguise them as toys for kids.

I wheeled along after Lorene, wondering why her face was puffy and red although I should have guessed. She slumped down at the kitchen table, her elbows beside the steam engines, and in-between crying jags, she said that once again her husband had called—clearly wasted—from a bar three states away to say he'd be gone another day or two seeing old biker friends. When he's not on it, his Harley's disassembled in the drive while he tinkers and pokes at it, revving it up and shutting it down.

"Just wait and see. He'll come home with another extra helmet," she said. "We got two left over from the girls he met on his last trips. He's a stickler for helmets, and too cheap to leave them behind."

I picture her husband astraddle the Harley, his black leather torso tilted forward, pumping away at the gas. Some woman wearing the new helmet will have her bare arms wrapped around his waist, her cheek against his leather shoulder. Lorene was probably imagining the exact same thing. "Have any heartbreak music?" she said. "Joni Mitchell. Or better yet, Tanya Tucker."

For a while, I was busy wheeling around offering her Kleenex, popping beer cans, sorting through CDs. Finally I shooed the cats away from my chair so I could get close enough to Lorene to pat her somewhere for comfort. I pulled up beside her like we were sitting on one of those fancy S-shaped loveseats you see in period movies—her kitchen chair facing one way and me on wheels facing the other. Then I twisted around toward her and rubbed her shoulders.

You can't rub someone forever. Soon I'm smoothing her fuzzy pink sweater, pushing her hair to one side of her neck, smelling the fruity sweetness of her shampoo. Then I got curious.

PAMELA PAINTER

I got curious about her hair. I wondered how her long hair would feel wrapped around my hand, sort of shaped against my palm and held in place by my thumb. I remember lifting her hair and twining it slowly around my hand. It was warm, heavy, more flexible than a cat's tail.

Lorene probably hadn't given me enough credit either. Credit for the curiosity I was now displaying. I was probably the guy in the wheelchair down the hall, always home, stocked up with butter, sugar and eggs, someone to baby sit little Lorene when she had an earache and couldn't go to school. I often leave my door cracked open, an invitation for company. People passing by in the hall come in and visit, complain about the ice and snow keeping us all inside or the government's plans to move the post office to the outskirts of town. Lorene saves her mending for watching HBO, or the World Series and the Academy Awards with me.

Next thing I knew, she turned around, slowly so as not to pull her hair out of my hand. Then she leaned toward me and put her hands on my shoulders, her thumbs warm inside my shirt collar.

We kissed.

What happened afterwards, well, it worked.

Lorene and I carried on the whole year she was separated till she gave her husband an ultimatum about what she called his booze, bikes, and babes and he came through. He's in AA now and trying to keep it tight. Got a job in Ohio at the Ford plant. He never knew about us—probably always pictured me in my wheelchair like I always pictured him on his Harley. Sure I hated to see her move away, but it was good they stayed together for little Lorene. And I put what Lorene taught me to good use.

I started looking for that spark of curiosity that kept a woman talking to me—a ditsy waitress at Reach-for-Ribs, the wholesaler who represents my toys, the bookmobile librarian (we're both on wheels I told her). The women were always someone I'd known a while and it didn't happen right away, but rather as a result of a little friction, a little heat. I respected that spark and when I could, I fanned it into flame. I had some wild affairs. Ordered blue satin sheets from a catalog, worked out with weights, changed the cat litter more often. The guys, pretty soon they knew to call before dropping in. They'd stop by my row at the movies for an introduction, honk when they saw some woman at the self-serve pumping unleaded into my van.

Trouble is. Now there's one wants to get married.

Her name's Maddy and she manages the drugstore next to Kozak's hardware. Wants us to start a Chamber of Commerce here in town. She has violet eyes, freckles, a good body, cooks, and gives me great ideas for my toys. When she left this morning she said "We've been going together almost a year."

"You mean sitting together," I said, wheeling over to my worktable. Turning my back.

"That isn't like you, Cady," she said, coming around to face me over a row of half-painted trucks.

She's right, but all this marriage talk has me nervous. Yesterday, I filled an order for trains when the store wanted dump trucks.

"I'll think about it," I said, looking up. We kissed. "Spaghetti tonight."

She laughed. "You think about it, and tonight I'll tell you what to say." She waved from the door. Someday I will paint a room the violet of her eyes. First, I need to study them a bit longer.

She says I love her.

I let her say it.

She says she loves me.

That's harder. It took me a while to credit curiosity. Now I got to learn to credit love.

Chance Encounter at LAX

Dear X,

Your plane about to leave; my plane about to leave. Each for a different coast. Final boarding calls minutes away. Only time enough for two glasses of ice water in a bar that is not scheduled to open for another hour, served by a sympathetic bartender alert to the minutes passing. What did we talk about? There was no time to ask about your twins, are they still speaking only to each other, to ask if you still reread James every summer or who you are reading now, and when did you gain weight, is your dean still obsessed with outcomes assessment, does your mother-in-law still add to your tie collection every year, do you still wear a tie, were you wearing a tie that day? How new is your computer or do you still write by hand? Did you make the move from violin to fiddle? Do you still dislike Penderecki? Who chose the cover of your latest book? Do you still ask for a Tanqueray martini with three olives? Doodle Escher-like sketches on reports and cocktail napkins? Are your house plants still only cacti? Did you give away the puppies from the next litter? Do you remember the time—? Do you recall the way—? Do you ever wish—?